A Note to Parents and Caregivers:

Read-it! Readers are for children who are just starting on the amazing road to reading. These beautiful books support both the acquisition of reading skills and the love of books.

The RED LEVEL presents familiar topics using common words and repeating sentence patterns.

The BLUE LEVEL presents new ideas using a larger vocabulary and varied sentence structure.

The YELLOW LEVEL presents more challenging ideas, a broad vocabulary, and wide variety in sentence structure.

The GREEN LEVEL presents more complex ideas, an extended vocabulary range, and expanded language structures.

When sharing a book with your child, read in short stretches, pausing often to talk about the pictures. Have your child turn the pages and point to the pictures and familiar words. And be sure to reread favorite stories or parts of stories.

There is no right or wrong way to share books with children. Find time to read with your child, and pass on the legacy of literacy.

Adria F. Klein, Ph.D.
Professor Emeritus
California State University
San Bernardino, California

Managing Editor: Bob Temple
Creative Director: Terri Foley
Editor: Brenda Haugen
Editorial Adviser: Andrea Cascardi
Copy Editor: Laurie Kahn
Designer: Melissa Voda
Page production: The Design Lab
The illustrations in this book were prepared digitally.

Picture Window Books
5115 Excelsior Boulevard
Suite 232
Minneapolis, MN 55416
1-877-845-8392
www.picturewindowbooks.com

Printed in the United States of America.

Library of Congress Cataloging-in-Publication Data
Blair, Eric.
The fisherman and his wife / by Jacob and Wilhelm Grimm ; by Eric Blair ;
illustrated by Todd Ouren.
p. cm. — (Read-it! readers fairy tales)
Summary: The fisherman's greedy wife is never satisfied with the wishes granted her by an
enchanted fish.
ISBN 1-4048-0317-3 (Library Binding)
[1. Fairy tales. 2. Folklore—Germany.] I. Grimm, Jacob, 1785-1863. II. Grimm, Wilhelm,
1786-1859. III. Ouren, Todd, ill. IV. Fisherman and his wife. English. V. Title. VI. Series.
PZ8.B5688Fi 2004
398.2—dc22   2003014005

The Fisherman and His Wife

A Retelling of the Grimms' Fairy Tale

By Eric Blair
Illustrated by Todd Ouren

Content Adviser:
Kathy Baxter, M.A.
Former Coordinator of Children's Services
Anoka County (Minnesota) Library

Reading Advisers:
Adria F. Klein, Ph.D.
Professor Emeritus, California State University
San Bernardino, California

Susan Kesselring, M.A.
Literacy Educator
Rosemount-Apple Valley-Eagan (Minnesota) School District

Picture Window Books
Minneapolis, Minnesota

About the Brothers Grimm

To help a friend, brothers Jacob and Wilhelm Grimm began collecting old stories told in their home country of Germany. Events in their lives would take the brothers away from their project, but they never forgot about it. Several years later, the Grimms published their first books of fairy tales. The stories they collected still are enjoyed by children and adults today.

Once upon a time, there was a poor fisherman. He lived with his wife in a tiny hut by the sea.

Each day, the fisherman went down
to the sea and cast his line into the water.
One day, the fisherman caught a big fish.

"Please let me go," the fish said. "I'm not a real fish. I'm really a prince under a magic spell. I wouldn't taste very good."

"I'd let a talking fish go anyway,"
the surprised fisherman said. He let
the fish swim away.

That night, the fisherman went home
to his wife. He told her the story
of the talking fish.

"Did you make a wish?" she asked.
The fisherman shook his head no.
"Such a fish could give you anything
you want," his wife said. "Why not ask
for a nice place for us to live?"

The fisherman went down to the water
and called, "Fishy, fishy in the sea!"

When the fish swam up, it asked,
"What do you want?"

The fisherman said, "My good wife says
I should wish for something because I let
you go. She wants a nicer place to live."

"Go home," said the fish. "She already has it."

12

The fisherman found his wife in a cottage
with a living room, bedroom, and kitchen.
"Are you happy now?" he asked.

"Let me think about it," was all she would say.

A few days later, the fisherman's wife said,
"This house and yard are very small.
It would be nice to live in a castle.
Go to the fish, and make another wish."

14

The fisherman thought it was wrong
to make another wish, but he did
as his wife ordered. The fisherman called
the fish. The fish swam up and asked,
"What do you want?"

The fisherman answered, "My good wife
wants to live in a castle."

"Go home," said the fish. "She already has it."

The fisherman found his wife
in a beautiful castle. Fine china
and food covered golden tables.
Crystal chandeliers hung from the ceilings,
and carpets covered the floors.

Behind the castle was a garden
with flowers, trees, and wild animals.
"Are you happy now?" asked the fisherman.

"Let me think about it," his wife said.

The next morning, the wife asked,
"Wouldn't you like to be king?"
The fisherman shook his head no.
"Tell the fish I want to be queen,"
his wife said.

Even though he thought it was wrong,
the fisherman went to the water and cried,
"Fishy, fishy in the sea!"

The fish asked, "What do you want?"

The fisherman answered, "My good wife wants to be queen."

"Go home," said the fish. "She's already the queen."

The fisherman went home and found
a palace with soldiers, drums, and trumpets.
He saw his wife wearing a gold crown
and sitting on a throne.

"Tell the fish I want to be the empress," the wife said.

"That's impossible," said the fisherman. "There's only one empress."

"Tell the fish," his wife ordered.

23

Even though he knew it was wrong,
the fisherman went to the water and cried,
"Fishy, fishy in the sea!"

The fish asked, "What do you want?"

The fisherman answered, "My good wife wants to be the empress."

"Go home," said the fish. "She's already the empress."

The fisherman found his wife
in an even larger, fancier palace.
She sat on a golden throne and wore
a crown of gold and rubies.

"How does it feel to be the empress?"
he asked.

"Go back to the fish, and tell him I want
to be like God," his wife said.

"But, my dear wife," said the fisherman, "there's only one God."

His wife would only say, "Go down, and talk to the fish."

There was a terrible storm, but the fisherman went down to the sea. Even though he knew it was wrong, he called to the fish. The fish asked, "What do you want?"

The wind blew, the lightning flashed, and the thunder crashed. The fisherman answered, "My good wife wants to be like God."

"Go home," said the fish. "Your wife asks for too much. Now she's back in the hut by the sea." The fisherman went home to his wife in the tiny hut by the sea, and there they live to this very day.

Levels for *Read-it!* Readers

Read-it! Readers help children practice early reading skills
with brightly illustrated stories.

Red Level: Familiar topics with frequently used words and repeating patterns.

Blue Level: New ideas with a larger vocabulary and a variety of language structures.

Little Red Riding Hood, by Maggie Moore 1-4048-0064-6

The Three Little Pigs, by Maggie Moore 1-4048-0071-9

Yellow Level: Challenging ideas with an expanded vocabulary and a wide variety of sentences.

Cinderella, by Barrie Wade 1-4048-0052-2

Goldilocks and the Three Bears, by Barrie Wade 1-4048-0057-3

Jack and the Beanstalk, by Maggie Moore 1-4048-0059-X

The Three Billy Goats Gruff, by Barrie Wade 1-4048-0070-0

Green Level: More complex ideas with an extended vocabulary range and expanded language structures.

The Brave Little Tailor, by Eric Blair 1-4048-0315-7

The Bremen Town Musicians, by Eric Blair 1-4048-0310-6

The Emperor's New Clothes, by Susan Blackaby 1-4048-0224-X

The Fisherman and His Wife, by Eric Blair 1-4048-0317-3

The Frog Prince, by Eric Blair 1-4048-0313-0

Hansel and Gretel, by Eric Blair 1-4048-0316-5

The Little Mermaid, by Susan Blackaby 1-4048-0221-5

The Princess and the Pea, by Susan Blackaby 1-4048-0223-1

Rumpelstiltskin, by Eric Blair 1-4048-0311-4

The Shoemaker and His Elves, by Eric Blair 1-4048-0314-9

Snow White, by Eric Blair 1-4048-0312-2

The Steadfast Tin Soldier, by Susan Blackaby 1-4048-0226-6

Thumbelina, by Susan Blackaby 1-4048-0225-8

The Ugly Duckling, by Susan Blackaby 1-4048-0222-3